TWO SHORT STORIES

by Michael G Hoback

DORRANCE PUBLISHING CO
EST. 1920
PITTSBURGH, PENNSYLVANIA 15238

Dorrance Publishing Co
585 Alpha Drive
Pittsburgh, PA 15238
Visit our website at *www.dorrancebookstore.com*

ISBN: 979-8-8872-9359-2
eISBN: 979-8-8872-9859-7

SECOND CHANCE

*Author's Note: I write only what comes to me and never to hurt someone.

"Breathtaking" is the only correct phrase to use in what is the experience just by simple eye vision alone.

To walk beside or near this large freshwater lake is to some food for the soul. Some things in this world you have to see to believe. This lake is actually North America's largest Alpine Lake. The lake's waters are crystalline clear and the sun's rays make unusual patterns in the water. Except in the deep depth of course, you can see to the bottom.

The many colors are amazing to see. Not only in the lake, but also in the surrounding stands of pine and other tree species, which are actually comforting in a way. There is also a calming feeling of peace and quiet in the solitude of being surrounded by mountains that stay snow-capped almost year round.

Everywhere you look it's like looking at a museum quality painting. The countless boulders of various sizes act as if they are an endless army of guarding sentinels.

Mark Twain himself wrote about his visit to Lake Tahoe.

Many people from all over the world come here to visit and never forget the experience.

Not all the roads are paved; some are still dirt only.

A visitor is walking a dirt road now.

It is a woman. She is tall somewhere around forty in age but looks younger. Her beauty is startling. Her hair is an off blond and parted perfectly in the middle. Its length is just to her shoulders and cannot hide the sparkling diamonds hanging from her ears. Her Hollywood quality makeup application enhances her large hazel eyes and her perfectly sculptured nose. Her lips have light red lipstick and bright white teeth behind them. She could very well be a model or actress.

The business suit she is wearing is by Gucci; its navy blue and incredibly expensive. Her high heels are black and held in place on her feet by a type of spider web. Her walk is full of confidence but unhurried. She walks awhile and stops and looks around.

Her eyes and facial expression betray what the surrounding area is doing to her.

Awestruck.

Her walk for the last hour and a half has been relaxing. Calmness has taken hold of her for the first time in many years. She actually does indeed find it soothing to her soul here.

Countless appointments, meetings, business calls, and lawyer conferences are forgotten.

Known internationally, she has a reputation for laughing easily and often. But she hasn't had a good laugh in many weeks. Her heart has felt...hollow.

Now something has changed.

With what she is seeing here on Lake Tahoe, it has had an effect on her.

Life here is without the noises of a major city or a large group of people chattering away like busy honey bees. Her very being is finding a healing and calming peace.

Countless hiking trails she finds or sees, but none has she even thought about attempting to scale. The dirt road has somehow called to her to stay her route and continue looking at the peace around her.

Finally her dirt road meets up with a paved road and she goes ahead and steps onto it but slows down even more. She is afraid the experience she is having will end and doesn't want the old to return.

Looking into the water's edge she sees fish swimming in the shallows. Birds are singing all around and a large falcon-like bird is up high in the sky circling in the air currents. Many clouds are in the sky but cannot hide a bright sun.

This is indeed another world.

The woman finds the road gradually going downhill closer to the water. After nearly a mile walk the road leads to a two-story log cabin on the edge of the lake.

It is magnificent.

The actual house looks to be made of some type of cedar. A large stone fireplace is sticking up out of the roof. The few surrounding trees in the neatly kept yard are full of birdhouses and bird feeders.

She walks closer.

The large deck goes all around the house and looks to be maybe some type of unusual hardwood. Tiger wood maybe. The deck railings are Douglas Fir. But the roof is some type of unusual modern grayish shingles. The house is neither too small nor too big. It's like a dream come true for someone.

The woman actually considers walking on, but something pulls her closer to the house. Two vehicles are parked out front. A metallic blue F150 Ford pickup truck from the early 70s in mint shape and a cherry red 78 Chevy Nova car. The car looks as well kept as the truck.

Beautiful.

With no fear she steps up onto the deck and walks on up to the custom made huge double doors. Both have an incredible woodwork of fish and deer around the thick glass insert. She peers in and sees a middle aged Caucasian male sitting at a large desk in a living room. He is writing in a simple notebook surrounded by a lot of books.

The room is made entirely of wood including all the furniture. It's like a house from another century. A few cushions are seen, though. It all evokes a simple type of comfort.

Behind the sitting man is a large stone fireplace. Above that is a large elk's head with a massive set of antlers. On each side of the fireplace are two big rock shelves full of firewood. The floor looks to be made of reclaimed hardwood that was hand cleaned to keep it looking as rustic as possible. Also there are timbered rough hewn posts with a vaulted ceiling above showing a Brazilian Cherry King Post Truss. But there are several modern black ceiling fans hanging from the ceiling.

A very modern kitchen can also be seen in the background.

Again it's like something propels her to move closer and raise her right hand and knock onto the door's thick glass.

The man looks up and the two look at each other and their eyes lock. After several seconds the woman smiles and finds herself waving at the man for some reason. He stands and walks over quickly opening up the rustic door.

"Car troubles miss?"

The man's speech has some sort of faint accent to it.

"Yes. I'm sorry to bother you love."

The woman's speech is some type of British.

"No problem."

"Do I know you sir? You look familiar."

"No. Never met you before."

The two stare at each other.

The man is around forty years of age. Brownish blond hair and a medium build. He is wearing blue jeans, a white shirt, and some kind of new very white tennis shoes. He is very smooth shaven.

The woman tries to notice the man's eye color, but he steps to the side and beckons her inside.

"You can call someone or I can take you into town. It's only like a thirty minute drive."

"That'll be fine," she answers as she steps inside.

The door closes.

"I'll be right back. I'll get my wallet and keys."

As he walks out of the view the woman can't help me but look around.

A lot of simple wooden bookshelves can be found everywhere in the room. All are full of books. Most of the framed art on the walls are of wildlife scenes, cowboy and/or Native American scenes. The desk has a lot of papers scattered about too. In one corner by the door is a fly fishing rod.

The man returns.

"You a reporter?"

"Lord no miss, I'm a writer."

The two walk out the door and the man locks it behind them. He escorts her to the truck, opens it for the lady, and closes it before then stepping into the driver's seat. Inside, the truck looks and smells brand new. Both put on their seatbelts. The man turns the key and starts the engine. It comes to life immediately and sounds powerful.

"I forgot to offer you something to eat or drink. I'm sorry."

"I'm fine."

Man drives the truck out of his driveway and onto the road.

"Are you sure we haven't met love?"

The man laughs. "No. I THINK I would remember you love."

Both laugh.

No more talk for awhile. The man drives and the woman looks around everywhere.

"It's beautiful here."

"Very peaceful too. I can hear myself think here."

"Want to use my cell phone to call your family?"

"No it's just me."

"No husband or kids?"

"No he left to find himself."

"I'm sorry."

"It's ok, I should not have married him. It was for all the wrong reasons."

"I'm sorry."

"It's ok love....I should have married a man years ago before I became very successful in my career."

"I'm sorry."

She simply shakes her head this time,

"Was that guy a nice guy?"

"Oh yes. He was a simple kind of guy. He loved to read and write. I didn't bother to ask him to come with me. After three years together I thought I knew him well enough to decide for him that he wouldn't want to make a life with a woman who would be gone for many weeks at a time all over the bloody world. So I just broke up with him."

"It happens honey, and I'm SURE he misses you still."

Both laugh again.

No more talking until the truck finds itself stopping at one of the best hotels in the area.

"Find that guy miss and give him another chance. Maybe he's a writer now living near a lake."

Both laugh at this as the lady opens her door and steps out. She finds herself actually waving goodbye to the driver and then walking on into the motel's huge lobby.

The Ford truck leaves and gets back onto the main road. The driver picks up speed; it's as if he is running from an unforgettable memory, and his jaw line tightens.

He turns on the radio to an oldies station and a song by Sarah McLachlan is beginning to play.

Make me a witness
Take me out
Out of darkness
Out of doubt
I won't weigh you down with good intentions

Won't make fire out of clay or other inventions
Will we burn in heaven
Like we do down here...

The man has tears falling from both eyes now; no matter how strongly he fights it.

Back at the hotel the woman has signed in at the hotel, booked their best penthouse, and is walking through the penthouse door. And now she is realizing neither she nor the man that brought her here know the other's name. Neither even bothered to ask.

Too late now.

She picks up the room phone and calls a trusted friend and agent she has had for ten years.

"I'm ok love just car trouble."

"Why did you go to Lake Tahoe?"

"I heard it was beautiful and they were right."

A moment of silence.

"Your ex-husband's lawyer called; he wants more living expenses money."

"I'm not surprised."

"Call your lawyer?"

"Yes."

"Need anything else?"

"Look up an address for me. It's probably somewhere in England. An old friend of mine."

"OK."

The agent is given a name and a last known address.

After eating an early dinner the woman takes a shower and goes on to bed. Her dreams are of a house on Lake Tahoe and the face of a man she can't recall where she has seen before today.

The next morning the woman awakens up a little past 9 A.M. and her eyes are crusted over heavily and a little sore. Having trouble seeing, she goes back to the bathroom and decides to jump into the shower. After spraying off her body she lets the warm water fall onto her face, especially her eyes. She reaches up and finds a crusty like film that is over both her eyes and immediately both eyes shed the film and it quickly goes down the drain.

She steps out of the shower and quickly dries off. After wiping off her face she finds her eyesight is now different. It's clearer and more focused. She calls the front desk and makes arrangements for fresh clothes and some makeup. Now she calls back her agent.

"I triple checked the info you gave me dear, but the man in question is not living in England now, but in the United States. And in Lake Tahoe, Nevada no less than thirty minutes from your hotel."

What the bloody hell?

After calling the front desk again for a driver or taxi she eats a small breakfast and gets dressed quickly. She arrives at the lobby's front desk flawless. Her hair is parted perfectly; her makeup looks incredible again, and she is dressed this time in tight Gloria Vanderbilt blue jeans and a man's expensive white dress shirt. Diamonds hang from her ears again and she is wearing the same black high heels too.

Her ride is the night kitchen manager who feels honored to be her driver in his little Toyota Scion.

"I know exactly where that road is miss. We'll find it together for you."

The driver drives his car fast and it's not long before the woman stops looking everywhere like a tourist and instead looks down at her feet.

Her mind is ablaze with thoughts of scenarios, rendezvous, lover spats, dreams, and love making from a decade earlier. Old ambitions are remembered too. All seem a million miles away.

"This is it miss."

Without looking at her surroundings the woman gets out the car as driver announces rather loudly.

"I can't wait to tell my wife who I chauffeured for today!"

As soon as the door is closed the driver races away beeping his horn.

With a somewhat bewildered look, the woman turns to look at the destination her driver has brought her to. Immediately her breathing stops, it's the very log cabin she was at yesterday!

Oh bloody hell!!!

She stands not moving as a dozen questions run through her head. Her hands shake a little as she walks unsteadily toward the familiar cabin. She begins to hear music and the closer she gets to the beautiful door once again the more she can discern the words being spoken. The voice is female and beautiful too.

Oh Lord, Love thy will be done
Since I have found you, my life has just begun
And I see all of your creations as one perfect complex
None less beautiful or more special than the next
We are all blessed and so wise to accept
Thy will, Love be done

She grits her teeth and looks inside like the day before, but he is not at the desk this time.

The same man is sitting in a wooden chair in front of the huge unlit fireplace. In his hand is a large bottle of beer, a Miller 40 half full. He gives off a vibe of being very tired.

She just glances at his face and instantly gasps for a breath she hasn't taken since setting her first step onto the deck. This time she recognizes the man!

Why she didn't yesterday puzzles her greatly.

That lost lover!

That lost lover from over ten years ago. The one she has dreamed about off and on forever!

Again something pushes both her arms to loudly slap her open palms against the door glass. The man turns, their eyes lock, and she backs away from the door. She is nearly ten feet away from the cabin door when the man opens the door and steps out onto the deck.

She can see his eyes now; they are a bright green.

He stops just a few feet from her.

The woman begins to cry.

"I thought I somehow recognized you yesterday!"

The man begins to cry too.

"I've missed you so much love."

The man nods his head.

Sobbing now the woman drops to the floor and sits; instantly the man joins her holding her in his arms. She returns the embrace.

"I thought I meant nothing to you so when my writing really took off I came to America and wrote under another name. I came here to Lake Tahoe for the peaceful solitude I prefer now."

"I've never cared for reading love."

"I know."

"Why didn't you tell me who you were yesterday?"

Both are still crying.

"I wanted you to make the choice for yourself."

The lady wipes away her tears and the two kiss like they did many years ago.

When the kiss ends the man looks the woman directly in her eyes.

"This time I don't want any kind of misunderstanding. I want to spend the rest of my life happily wrapped around one of your fingers. Or just be merciful and blow my brains out with a pistol. I've felt hollow for just too long now. Is that clear?"

"Yes love."

"I'll go with you anywhere in the world you need to go. And we'll make this log cabin our home base if that's ok with you."

No answer is needed. Both their eyes say what the other needs to hear.

They both smile like they haven't in a long time.

The two embrace again with nothing more to say and slowly all tears stop. A slight breeze arrives and envelops the two with a soothing coolness.

Twenty minutes later the two are embracing still and not talking.

They hold each other tightly as if their very souls need each other or they shall die.

Sometimes..Love will make a way.

Lake Tahoe carries on as it has for eons. Bright skies, emerald clear waters, countless sentinels and countless birds busy surviving while they sing or chirp. A type of happiness is in the air today.

RAINMAKER

*Author's Note: I am not an Odinist, but if you, the reader, are, you might like this short story.

The rains have not fallen in nearly two months. Everything is drying up. Most people around this part of the state have lawns that look like they have the mange. Farmers are worried the most. Not knowing if they are going to have any crops to sell to their buyers. Most of their money is tied up in loans soon due at the end of each harvest.

The weather hasn't been this unpredictable in years. Even climate scientists are perplexed.

The sitting President of this United States of America just last week asked the entire nation for a day of prayer.

"Let all believers of any god they choose to believe in gather tomorrow in friendship at noon to pray for rain to fall."

And it happened all over the United States for one day. Many people of countless faiths came together to pray to their god of choice for some rain.

Nothing happened.

Several days passed.

Then a third generation wheat farmer wrote a piece in the local newspaper asking for a "rainmaker" to come forward. The farmer actually offered five thousand dollars to anyone that will come to his dying farm and make the rain fall. The farmer wrote that he had emptied out a small savings and would hand it out only COD after the rain falls.

A local news station caught wind of the article in the paper and made it their top story on the six o'clock news the next day.

Then CNN and Fox caught the story. Facebook was diluted with the story quickly. The whole world had an eye then on the old farmer and his request for a rainmaker and his offer to pay out five thousand cash if the rainmaker was successful.

"Saturday Night Live" on NBC even did a skit on the story.

It was a laugh for all.

But then that local paper printed the fact that the old farmer was a recent widower with no living children to be found.

The wife had recently died of a type of very painful cancer. And his only child, a son, had died roughly two years earlier in a war in a far away land. He had been a Marine Lance Corporal. His funeral had been closed casket, but the father had insisted later that night that the funeral director open up the casket so he could verify himself the body therein.

That's when the laughter ended.

The following Saturday evening a female CNN reporter and her crew showed up at the farmers' house to ask for an update.

"Has someone accepted your offer sir?"

"Yes," the farmer replies. "Someone called me last night. But they wanted only five dollars and not the five grand. A strong female voice said they'd be here this Wednesday by car at noon sharp in a metallic blue car."

"Sir I hope they are successful," the reporter responds.

"I hope so too young lady; my farm is about dead."

Pretty soon the whole world has heard of this statement. Every kind of news source on earth of many languages told of the impending rain-maker's arrival.

A famous Hollywood director announced he'd pay an additional one hundred thousand dollars of his own money if the rainmaker did indeed make rain and was privately considering a made for TV movie.

Las Vegas stepped into the soup and started taking bets. Some of the bets were outrageous and many were anonymous.

The president called in to "The View" and said he himself would be near a TV noon Wednesday.

Come Tuesday morning a lot of news people and interested people begin arriving. It's not long before the farmer has to call in the local sheriff to keep people off his property. He tells the sheriff, "I don't want the newest version of Woodstock on my property anywhere."

Soon the nosy people begin standing just off his property, along his many fences, in the surrounding woods, and some spectators even rented helicopters or planes. A lot of giant news cameras are all around too. Some news crews set up their cameras on top of their vans.

But the farmer insists that the sheriff not chase off anyone. Not the press or the hundreds of spectators.

Tuesday evening, the weathermen on all local TV stations began informing the public just how much rain would be needed from the rainmaker.

And nine o'clock Wednesday morning Kansas State Troopers have arrived to help with the crowds and the traffic. Logistics are a nightmare when nothing is planned for at all when something like this is never thought of to begin with.

Many victims of heat stroke are taken away by ambulance.

Nearer to noon more helicopters and planes are flying overhead. All roads are demanded to be clear of all traffic by the state troopers.

Then at 11:55 A.M. something happens. A mile down the road a metallic blue car suddenly comes flying out from a rarely used dirt road onto the main paved road. The car is some type of New York taxi from the 1950s, not copied in any basic design in many decades. Its tires are white-walled wide Mag tires. All its windows are tinted and there are multiple tall radio antennas. The front license plate matches the rear one. In large letters is one word, 'ASGARD."

The car is absolutely spotless and everything shines. Its high performance engine roars with sheer power like it wants to be set free. It dual exhausts shoot flames.

The car pulls onto the farmer's property exactly at noon sharp. The distance from the gate to the farmer's house is nearly 250 yards. On both sides of the road are the farmer's withering crops. The car comes to within fifty feet of the house and suddenly stops. The car is put in park and the engine is cut off.

The driver's door opens.

The driver steps out.

Camera flashes are flashing everywhere from around the farm. News cameras are recording the scene as the reporters are trying their best to describe the scene to the home viewers as professionally and accurately as possible.

A woman steps out.

But she immediately impresses everyone and gets everyone's attention.

She is tall, over six feet and dressed boldly in a white Gucci women's business suit. No high heels here, but instead high heeled boots with fur! Her face is almost like a mannequin model: perfect with no blemishes at all. Her hair is as startling dark as a raven's feather and long, well past her shoulders. And her lips are a bright red, almost like fresh blood. Her eyes from even a distance are a startling blue.

Closing her door the woman walks around the front of the car and something else is noticed.

She walks with authority and power.

This woman still has the walk of a female but with a type of power exuding from her. Under her clothes people would find her quite muscular. Only a chosen few are allowed to see her softness. Reaching the back door on the passenger side of the vehicle she opens up the door and steps back.

A giant of a man steps out as cameras are again flashing from every direction.

The man looks like he just stepped away from a Hollywood Viking movie. He too is well over six foot tall, but his great muscular body is quickly apparent from the flimsy sleeveless shirt of chainmail covering his chest. His pants look to be leather-like and his boots too, but they are tied off tightly with silk-like black bands of some type.

The big man begins walking out into the field.

His face is strong; toughness is seen immediately in him. His long hair is red and his beard is too. Both hands are encased in some type of metal gloves and his head has a metal helmet with great bull horns sticking out from each side in a slight forward curve with a sharp point on top. Around his massive shoulders is a great cloak made from some type of animal fur. Finally what is noticed is what is in his right hand. A great rock hammer of some kind, bound with leather strips around the handle length and a leather throng also hanging loosely from the end.

The woman closes the rear door and walks back quickly to her driver's seat and closes that door as a strong wind begins to be felt.

When the red haired giant reaches roughly the middle of the field he has entered he stops and looks at the farmer. The sky is no longer cloudless; grayish clouds are gathering quickly and the wind is growing stronger still.

The giant's face betrays nothing

He is quite calm; greatly at peace.

But then his jaw sets tightly and countless news crews describe what happens next.

"The sky like ripped itself open and this giant of a man raised his hammer and a bolt of lightning came down from the sky and strikes the hammer!"

"Sparks and smoke are everywhere!"

"The sky rumbles loudly and is alive with movement and lightning strikes everywhere!"

With his hammer still raised to the sky an ancient long forgotten language is spoken from his lips and countless more bolts fall from the sky above and strike the giant man's hammer! This man is smiling now, as if he is enjoying the experience. It's as if the great bolts of electricity are giving him a great charge!

"The wind is now blowing close to hurricane category!"

"Now lightening bursts forth from the hammer and strikes back upwards toward the sky!"

"Rain has begun to fall from the sky that looks like as if it has been literally ripped apart and an ocean of different colored clouds is churning now above us!"

Within seconds the rain begins to fall in great fury.

"The figure with the hammer seems to be enjoying what is happening! He is standing tall, legs wide apart, and looking at the sky as if he is seemingly directing a great orchestra....Now with both his arms stretched high above his head a great wind begins to blow."

"People are running for cover everywhere!"

Many climb into any vehicles that suddenly open their doors to them. Several are knocked to the ground by the scared crowds. Occasionally lightening falls from the sky to again strike the hammer. And some trees begin to topple, mostly pine trees and birch with their shallow roots. Several cameras and their crew are blown off the top of their vehicles.

The great red headed warrior drops his hands, but the storm continues. And he smiles a little as the old farmer runs as fast as he can back into his house. He closes the door and looks out a large side window. The sky continues to release large torrents of rain as if it was suddenly ordered to do so by a god.

The rain and strong winds affect everything and everyone, but the rainmaker stands tall and unmoving as if attached to the ground by a great magnate underneath him. Only his great fur cloak blows wildly around him blown by the winds.

As the farmer watches from inside his house a reporter tries to tell the public what is going on from a nearby barn. Her cameraman is in a nearby ditch trying to put the camera back together while standing knee high in churning water.

"This huge man has seemingly brought on this great rainstorm."

Other reporters are trying to describe the scene also.

"He is tall; nearly seven feet and very muscular. His hair and beard are red and he has a shiny metal cap on his head with great bull horns attached to each side and tilting a little forward like I guess a Viking helmet!"

"This being's clothing is simple. He wears a type of sleeveless gray chain mail on his upper body and his pants and fur lined boots are both leather and tied off with some kind of silk-like straps."

"Who is this being and what is he?"

"A loud crack of thunder just went off high above us here!"

The cameraman standing in the now waist high ditch gives up on rebuilding his camera in the pouring rain and carries the camera parts over to stand beside his reporter partner.

"This being has somehow just taken off from the ground and up into the sky somehow using his hammer to take flight," the female reporter yells into her microphone.

Her cameraman shakes his head. He knows his broken camera has stopped him from recording something incredibly wondrous and amazing for the posterity of the human race!

"What the hell is this?" yells another reporter nearby.

"Now this being with the hammer is flying over us from a high altitude. He seems to turn his body and the hammer responds and then turns him to that direction."

All eyes willing to battle the rain and the wind are watching the giant man fly all over the sky back and forth. If the people could see his face he has a smile and a twinkle-like shine to his eyes.

"Who the hell is this guy?" asks another reporter.

Similar questions are being asked by countless reporters all around the farm.

The red headed being arrives back to the spot he left from. His landing is loud and powerful. It seems to have no effect on the man. He turns to look back at the farmer staring out from his window. Raising his hammer, the giant yells something in the unknown ancient language again and the rains just immediately stop. Within a minute the sky is light blue, partially cloudy, and the sun is shining.

The man then bows his head a little to the farmer inside his house and turns, walking quickly back to a waiting car. By the time he reaches the car the driver with the long black hair is awaiting him with his door open. Cameras are flashing everywhere. The giant steps into the car and she closes the door.

The woman then turns and walks toward the house. The farmer steps outside and meets her maybe 10 feet from his front door. He is greatly impressed by her, not only by her face and incredible hair but also by her very walk. He has taken off his greatly worn red Ford cap out of respect.

The woman is tall, somewhere around six-four and a powerfully built body is noticed immediately behind the expensive clothing. She merely puts out her right hand saying nothing.

The old farmer pulls out a worn leather wallet and hands her a five dollar bill and she just turns and simply walks away.

"What is the rainmaker's name?" the farmer asks.

There is standing water everywhere for the eye to see.

The woman stops and half turns back toward the farmer

"His name is Thor," a beautiful but strong voice sounds from her lips. And then she turns and walks back to the car.

Starting up the vehicle, it is quickly back on the road as its windshield wipers wipe away the remaining water on the windshield. People, reporters, and law enforcement officers come running to the car. A change of gear, a sudden push on a gas petal, and the car takes off with flames shooting out the dual exhausts.

Later in the day satellites in earth's orbit will show the joint chiefs and the president that the car went down the road about a mile to a little used dirt road and disappeared in a cluster of trees shortly thereafter.

Many people in many countries have an endless amount of unanswered questions now. But many people also living in Scandinavia, Iceland, and Greenland are showing the world what a true Viking feast is like, as are parts of Russia.

www.ingramcontent.com/pod-product-compliance
Lightning Source LLC
Chambersburg PA
CBHW051339150726
47997CB00004B/1533